THERE'S A MOUSE IN GRANDMA'S HOUSE!

THERE'S A MOUSE IN GRANDMA'S HOUSE!

What Should We Do?

Heidi Lynn Studer & Grandson, Chetley Jae Tuman

ReadersMagnet, LLC

There's A Mouse In Grandma's House! What Should We Do?

Published in the United States of America
ISBN Paperback: 978-1-954371-60-6
ISBN eBook: 978-1-954371-61-3

ReadersMagnet, LLC
10620 Treena Street, Suite 230 | San Diego, California, 92131 USA
1.619.354.2643 | www.readersmagnet.com

Cover design by Kent Gabutin
Interior design by Renalie Malinao
Illustrated by Jebb Impok

There's a mouse in Grandma's house!
What should we do?

First, let's use our creative minds to
think and to explore

How we can get the mouse out of
Grandma's house

Unharmed and out the door

There's a mouse in Grandma's house!
What should we do?

Let's use a mop to whizz him out

And watch him roll and give a hop

There's a mouse in Grandma's house!
What should we do?

Let's leave some water in a cup

And when he is thirsty,
he'll take a big gulp

Just maybe he'll fall in
and get himself stuck

There's a mouse in Grandma's house!
What should we do?

Let's use a hockey stick to swish him
back and forth

Give it one bigger stride

And out the door he will glide

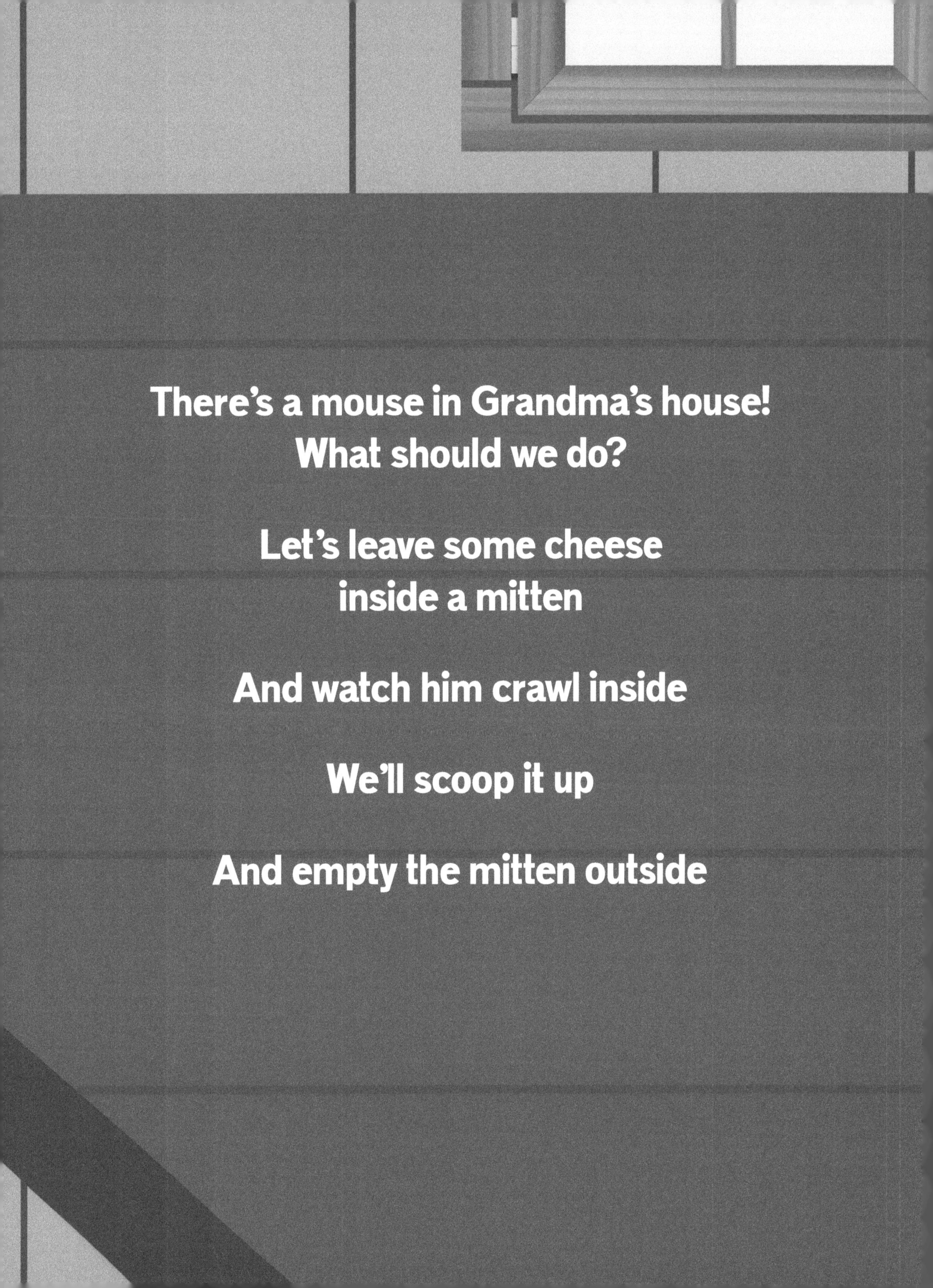

There's a mouse in Grandma's house!
What should we do?

Let's leave some cheese
inside a mitten

And watch him crawl inside

We'll scoop it up

And empty the mitten outside

There's a mouse in Grandma's house!
What should we do?

Let's try a shoebox

And turn it on its side

To him it may look like a cozy house

And build a nest inside

HOME

There's a mouse in Grandma's house!
What should we do?

Let's spread some peanut butter on a
slice of bread

And lay it on the counter

In hopes the mouse gets caught

before my little brother, Ed

There's a mouse in Grandma's house!
What should we do?

Let's sprinkle a path of
seeds on the floor

And watch the little mouse gobble
them up as he scampers out the door

There's a mouse in Grandma's house!
What should we do?

Let's fill a basket with some
socks and yarn

And just maybe the mouse
will come and darn

And while he darns, he'll fall asleep

While he sleeps, to the great outdoors
we will sneak.

There's a mouse in Grandma's
house! What should we do?

Let's find Grandma's fishing net

A different kind of mouse
trap we've set

When mouse comes out,
we'll scoop him up

Then flip him over and into
the grass he'll drop

There's a mouse in Grandma's house!
What should we do?

Let's set up our race car tracks

Run them to and fro

The mouse will jump on,
and have some fun

Sliding out the open window he will go

There's a mouse in Grandma's house!
What should we do?

At last, at last

We give a big shout

Tabby cat moved in

And mouse has moved out

Therefore, there is no more mouse in
Grandma's house!
Now, what should we do?

Now put your thinking caps on and have fun answering these questions:

1. If you had a mouse in your house, think about some cool ideas you would use to get the mouse out of your house.

2. Once the mouse is out of your house, what are some other fun and creative things you could do with your time?

3. Think about some things you could do to help someone else around their house.

10620 Treena Street, Suite 230
San Diego, California,
CA 92131 USA
www.readersmagnet.com
1.619.354.2643

www.ingramcontent.com/pod-product-compliance
Ingram Content Group UK Ltd.
Pitfield, Milton Keynes, MK11 3LW, UK
UKHW062002290726
14090UKWH00021B/1347

9 781954 371606